MULTICULTURAL READERS
SET 1

GHOST
BIKER

ANNE SCHRAFF

Artesian Press

P.O. Box 355 Buena Park, CA 90621

STANDING TALL MYSTERY SERIES
MULTICULTURAL READERS
SET 1

Project Editor: Carol E. Newell
Cover Illustrator: Fujiko
Cover Design: Tony Amaro
©2000 Artesian Press

ISBN 1-58659-082

Chapter 1

Kader Toma came streaking down the Coyote Mountain trail covered with dust and grime. He ground to a stop and took off his sunglasses.

"Kader! Even your teeth are dirty! The only thing clean is the skin around your eyes," Paloma laughed. "You look like a raccoon!"

"Man, this is so much fun," Kader said.

"Your brother says you're a fool, wasting your time on mountain biking. He says if you want to try out for a sport it should be football or basketball where the money is," Paloma said.

"Najor has dollar signs in front of his eyes," Kader said. "There is more to life than money. I put in plenty of hours helping my parents and Najor in the deli, but when I get time off, I want to have my kind of fun."

Paloma nodded. "My father is like Najor. All he talks about is money. We never have enough. Mom makes Halloween masks. Papa makes jewelry. But they never have enough money. Kader, when you come down the mountain like that, it looks so scary!"

"Life is scary, Paloma. We came to America because life was scary in the Gulf. But it's more scary here in some ways. The thing I'm least afraid of is riding my bike. On the streets, yeah, everybody is honking and trying to run you down. But out here in the hills, it's great. What's to be afraid of?" Kader said.

Paloma smiled. "I hate motorbikes because then you can't smell the wildflowers. But your mountain bike is nice and clean, Kader. All you need are strong muscles to make it go. I like that," she said.

Kader grinned. "Who knows, Paloma, maybe I'll get so good at this I'll end up in the Tour de France."

"What's that?" Paloma asked.

"The Super Bowl of biking. You get to bike in the Alps in Europe and finish in Paris. Greg LeMond won it once, you know," Kader said.

"Well, Kader, I gotta go to work. See you in school Monday," Paloma said.

"I'm sorry you have to work all the time. We don't get to see each other much," Kader said.

"Yeah. Well, at least it gets me out of the house so I don't hear my folks fighting about money. It's like even the walls yell all the time 'money, money, money!'" Paloma said, walking down to the road and pedaling off on her blue bike.

Kader walked his bike part way up

the hill, then climbed on for the gradual descent. The road down zigzagged among rocks and weeds, and Kader leaned forward, gripping the handlebars. It felt a little like flying must feel, he thought, with everything going by in a blur.

Kader was speeding down the hill when he heard someone behind him. A guy dressed all in black was riding a mountain bike. Kader didn't like the looks of the guy, so he put on more speed, bouncing over ruts and loose soil. The guy was gaining on him so Kader backtracked and climbed a grueling hill, hoping to lose the dark biker. Kader's thighs burned and his breath came in gasps, but his great strength proved too much for his pursuer. The other biker fell farther and farther back until, at the top of the hill, Kader lost him.

Kader biked down a back trail to where he'd parked his pickup truck. He felt uneasy in a way he'd never felt before. What did the guy want? You never knew these days—if some weirdo didn't like the color of your shirt or something.

Kader put his bike in the back of the pickup and headed for town. He glanced back across the hills that were covered with yellow mustard and mountain lilac. He saw nothing of the other biker. Kader shook his head and smiled to himself. Maybe the guy was a mirage! Maybe he wasn't ever there— a ghost biker. His face was sure pale enough to be a ghost.

Out on the highway, Kader glanced back one last time, and there he was— the black-suited, white-faced guy at the top of the hill staring at Kader.

Chapter 2

"You look a mess," Najor snapped when Kader came home. "Did you take a roll in the mud or what?"

"Nah. I was just enjoying myself in the hills. It's nothing a good hot bath won't wash off."

"Coach Bailey is asking guys to try out for the basketball team, Kader. You're good. Why don't you try for it?" Najor asked.

"Basketball bores me. I hate competitive sports. I get enough competition in the classroom. I want to enjoy myself when I play," Kader said.

Najor's eyes narrowed. He was younger than Kader, but he seemed more mature and practical sometimes.

"Basketball could get you a college scholarship," he said.

"Hey, Najor, something weird happened out in the hills today. A guy all in black with this smoky white face seemed to be chasing me. Can't figure it," Kader said, changing the subject from basketball.

"Some mountain bike freak. I think you're all a little nuts," Najor said.

"No, seriously. I just wondered if I had an enemy I didn't know about," Kader said.

"Paloma's old boyfriend, maybe," Najor said. "She used to hang out with Yoshia. He seemed to be a hot-tempered jerk, remember?"

"Yeah. He graduated from high school last year. Went on to college or something. I guess it could've been him, but Paloma never told me he still had a case on her," Kader said.

Kader showered and changed clothes. He was going to the school production of *Fiddler on the Roof* with Paloma. Her sister was playing Hodel.

As they drove towards San Bruno High, Kader told Paloma about the strange biker who followed him. "You don't think Yoshia has hard feelings about us going together, do you?" he asked her.

Paloma turned her head sharply. "You think Yoshia was the biker?" she asked.

"Well, I don't know. This guy seemed determined to chase me out of the hills. He was tall, with a gaunt face … a white face … like he wore makeup or something," Kader said.

"That could be Yoshia," Paloma said, frowning. "It might be something he would do. That's why I broke up with him. He was so possessive. It's like he thought he owned me totally. Yoshia is a good guy, but I got sick of having to report everything I did to him.…"

"Maybe he's trying to scare me off," Kader said.

"I'll call him tonight and tell him to stop it if he is," Paloma said.

The next day, when Kader returned to his favorite hills to ride his mountain bike, he saw no one around. Paloma had called Yoshia, and he denied being the ghost biker, but Paloma was still suspicious.

"Well," Kader said to himself as he unloaded his bike, "it's just me and the circling hawks today. And that's how I like it."

Kader climbed on his bike and started up the hill. When he got to the top he stood and looked around at the blue lupine, yellow daisies, and cream cups. He inhaled the warm, sweet air. Then, just before he began his downward plunge on the trail, someone fired a shot only a few feet from his head. The bullet hit a tree, splintering a branch.

Kader turned numb. He jumped on his bike and streaked down the hill, cold perspiration drenching his shirt. Somebody had *fired* at him! Somebody up here among the once-friendly brush and rocks actually fired at him!

Kader ran to his pickup and drove towards town, stopping at the sheriff's office.

"Lotta jerks do target practice out there," the deputy said. "Probably just a fool firing away."

"It wasn't *your* head that almost got shot off!" Kader protested. "I think he was firing at me!"

Chapter 3

Kader returned home frightened. He told his family what happened.

"You must stay away from that place," Mom said. "Somebody told me years ago bandits used to hide out on Coyote Mountain. The posse would follow them there and find their stolen gold."

"Mom, that was over a hundred years ago!" Kader cried.

"If you went out for basketball you wouldn't be fooling around in the mountains," Dad said.

"Yeah," Najor chimed in. "There's nobody shooting at the hoopsters."

"Some jerk is not going to scare me away from my favorite place," Kader snapped. "Anyway, if someone is out to get me, they'll come after me wherever I am!"

"But the one you call the ghost biker ... he is there in the hills. It's a bad place for you to be, son," Mom said.

Kader worked for four hours at the deli, then he drove to the college where Yoshia went. Paloma gave Kader the address of Yoshia's apartment. Kader figured if he took a good look at the guy he'd know if Yoshia was the biker.

Kader rang the bell and Yoshia answered. He was tall and gaunt. He could have been the ghost biker, but Kader wasn't sure. "Hi. I'm Kader Toma," Kader began.

"I've got nothing to say to you," Yoshia said, beginning to close the door. Kader stopped the door with his foot.

"Somebody has been harassing me," Kader said.

"Good," Yoshia said, "more power to 'em."

"Look, I'm not putting up with it," Kader said. "If it's you back off unless you want a visit from the sheriff."

"It's not me. If Paloma is stupid enough to go out with a guy like you then it's not my problem. You are biker bum whose parents own a tacky deli. I am going to be an engineer in my father's firm. So get your foot out of my door," Yoshia said.

Kader drove home, unsure of whether Yoshia was telling the truth or not. One thing was sure. Kader wasn't going to let this change his life. What good was it living in a free country if you couldn't ride your own bike in the hills when you wanted?

At school on Tuesday, Coach Bailey approached Kader. "Your brother tells me you're a pretty fair player, Kader. We need a tall center. How about it?"

"I just don't enjoy basketball," Kader

said.

"Lot of advantages in playing on a team, Kader. You learn a lot that helps you in life. Teamwork, hanging in there during the tough times," Coach Bailey pointed out.

"I know. I played when I was a freshman," Kader said.

Coach Bailey smiled wistfully. "That's before I was coach. I understand you were the high scorer in every game. You could put the San Bruno Bears in the winner's column, Kader. A boy like you on the team would make all the difference. How tall are you, Kader?"

"Six two," Kader said.

Coach Bailey whistled. "They say you hardly ever missed a free throw. I can believe it."

Kader looked at the coach's weary face. He'd never had a winning team that got into the playoffs. It was rumored that this would be his last year at San Bruno if he couldn't put a winning season together.

"Well, I'll think about playing, Coach," Kader said.

Coach Bailey slapped Kader on the back. "Good boy!"

When Kader got home, Najor was already stocking the deli shelves. A year younger than Kader, Najor loved sports, but he just wasn't good as a player. The best he could do was the intramural team.

"Maybe I'm going to play basketball after all," Kader said.

"All right!" Najor screamed.

A strange, unwanted thought came to Kader. Was it possible his own brother had tried to scare him off his mountain bike?

Chapter 4

"You really want me to play, don't you, Najor? Why? What's it to you?" Kader asked.

"Hey, big brother, is it such a crime to want a basketball star in the family?" Najor demanded.

Wednesday morning when Paloma opened her locker she screamed and jumped back. Kader was only a few feet away and came running. A white rat was crawling around inside Paloma's locker!

"Ooooh, I hate rats," Paloma groaned.

"I'll get it," Kader said. He used to have a pet rat when he was small.

"Ooooh, how can you touch it!"

Paloma cried.

"It's harmless. Here's another pet for Ms. Quigley in science," Kader said.

"Well, whoever stuck a rat in my locker didn't like me much," Paloma said.

Another girl walked over. "I saw that Yoshia guy in the hall a few minutes ago, Paloma. Your old boyfriend. I bet he knew your locker combination."

"Yeah, we shared library books, and we'd go in each other's lockers," Paloma said.

Kader hurried down the hall and got to the parking lot as Yoshia was getting in his car. Yoshia jumped into his sedan and took off with Kader following in his pickup. When Kader crowded the cream colored sedan with his battered pickup, Yoshia pulled over fast. He didn't want dents on his cream puff car.

"Hey, Yoshia, why are you stuffing

rats in Paloma's locker for?" Kader yelled when he came to Yoshia's window.

"You're nuts. I came to San Bruno to get a transcript," Yoshia said. "Now get your rust bucket outta my way."

"Yoshia, you bother Paloma or me again and I'm coming over to the college parking lot and spray painting the word 'jerk' all over your car."

Yoshia looked scared as he drove away.

At lunchtime, Kader noticed Najor, usually a loner, surrounded by a large group of kids. Kader wondered what Najor was doing to attract so much attention.

"Man," Danver Wilson was saying, "I'd give anything for that basketball."

Kader edged closer, finally spotting the basketball in Najor's hands. It had a lot of autographs on it.

"What've you got there, Najor?" Kader asked.

Najor's face turned red. "Ahh … just a basketball …" he mumbled.

Damien laughed. *"Just a basketball!* Oh, man, right! Just a basketball signed by the Chicago Bulls, all of them—the 1993 championship team, Michael Jordan and the rest!"

"Wow," Kader gasped, "where'd you get it, Najor?"

Najor looked strange. His eyes narrowed, and he looked guilty. "I won it," he said.

"You won it?" Kader asked. "Where? What fool bets something like that away?"

"Get off my back, Kader," Najor suddenly yelled. "It's none of your business, okay?"

After school, Kader put his bike in the back of the pickup and headed for the hills. He had an hour before he had to go work at the deli. He put on his helmet and climbed on his bike, starting up the hill. He paused at the top and looked around. No ghost biker in sight. Nobody tried to scare him by taking shots at him.

A cold, hard suspicion returned to Kader's heart. Had his own brother been behind the harassment to get Kader away from his favorite pastime and into the basketball team at San Bruno? Even Najor had no right to do something like that. Kader wouldn't stand for it. He intended to get at the truth if he had to beat Najor up to do it!

Chapter 5

Kader sailed down the trail feeling all the joy and exhilaration he always felt when he was biking. He'd never give it up. Even if he played on the basketball team he'd find time to do this, too.

Kader stomped into his house finding both his parents working at the deli and Najor doing homework in his room. "Najor, open up," Kader rapped on the door.

"I'm busy. I'm doing geometry," Najor snapped back.

"Open up or I'll bust down the door," Kader said.

Finally Najor opened the door. "I told you I was busy. You want me to flunk Geometry?"

"I went out to the hills just now and nobody was hassling me, Najor. No scary ghost biker chasing me. Nothing. Isn't it amazing that the harassment stops the minute I agree to play for the San Bruno Bears?" Kader said.

Najor shrugged. "So what's that supposed to mean?"

"It's simple, Najor. Just like geometry. Logic. I'm scared off the mountain so I got plenty of time now. I might as well play basketball. Then you turn up with a real trophy. A 1993 Chicago Bulls basketball—what's that add up to?" Kader asked.

"Man! Are you saying I was behind you being harassed? Your own brother? Man, you make me sick!" Najor shouted.

"Where'd you get the signed basketball, Najor?" Kader demanded, walking over and snatching it off the mantle.

"Put that back!" Najor cried. "That's

the best thing I ever got!"

Kader twirled the ball. "Where'd you get it?" he asked.

Najor jumped up and tried to get the ball away from Kader, but the much stronger, taller Kader blocked him. It was like in a basketball game. Nobody got the ball away from Kader Toma.

The Toma apartment was on the second floor. Down below in the streets a dozen boys played ball. It was twilight and the game was almost over. The window was open and Kader stood beside it, twirling the ball. "How long do you think this ball would last if I flipped it out the window, do you think? Think those boys down there could resist a ball signed by Mike and company?"

"Kader, I'll kill you!" Najor screamed.

"Tell me where you got it, or out it goes," Kader promised.

"Okay! Okay! Coach Bailey's son ... he talked to me ... he said his pop was really depressed about losing his coaching job at San Bruno. Tommy Bailey said if I could convince you to play for the Bears he'd give me his prize basketball. He said not to tell his Dad or anything," Najor said.

Kader still twirled the ball near the window. "Did you hire some clown to scare me off the mountain with that ghost biker outfit?"

"No, I swear I didn't!" Najor said. "I wouldn't do that. Not even for a 1993 Bulls' basketball, never!"

Kader tossed the basketball to his brother. "Okay. I'm sorry if I misjudged you. But I hate people messing with my life, okay?"

Najor stood there in silence, his basketball in hand. "You're still playing for the Bears, aren't you?"

"Yeah," Kader said. He went to his own room, showered and got dressed.

He'd take over the deli from his parents at four and work until seven-thirty.

Business was slow for the first twenty minutes, then a girl about thirteen came in. "A man said to give you this," she said, handing Kader a small white box. "You are Kader Toma, right?"

"Yeah," Kader said, taking the box. After the girl left he flipped it open. A small plastic skull lay on a bed of cotton. A neatly typed note said *Stay off Coyote Mountain or die.*

Chapter 6

Kader rushed from behind the counter. He had to find that girl who delivered the box. He had to find out where she got it. "Stop!" Kader shouted at the girl who was now far in the distance, hurrying along. She looked back, frightened, and began to run, vanishing into the darkness. Kader stared at the little plastic skull in his hand and returned to the deli.

Kader finished his three and a half hour stint at the deli and returned home. He'd decided not to mention the plastic skull to his parents. Why worry them? But late that night Kader quietly left the house and drove to Coyote Mountain. He parked the pickup down the road and walked down the brushy trail, binoculars in hand. He stopped every few minutes to listen and look. Someone was trying to chase him off this mountain. There had to be a reason.

Suddenly Kader heard a chopping sound—a pickaxe striking rock. Somebody was digging on the other side of the mountain. It wasn't where he usually rode his mountain bike, but it was close enough that his presence might have worried someone doing something illegal.

Kader moved slowly to the ridge, his back to the rocks. He made sure he stayed well in the shadows so he wouldn't be seen. Finally he saw a tall figure in the distance wielding a pickaxe. He'd chop the earth, then stoop, pick up a shovel and remove dirt, making a pile of it. It looked like the ghost biker, but Kader couldn't be sure. Each time the man struck the ground he made a soft, almost unearthly moan as if the digging was a great physical effort for him. Yet he continued, striking the earth, shoveling, then striking it again.

Kader turned and made his way back down the mountain. He'd drive to town and tell the police about the digger. Some unusual activity was taking place here on Coyote Mountain. Kader wanted it stopped. He wanted his mountain back.

Kader was picking his way back down the mountain towards his pickup truck when he let out a gasp. His truck was gone! His truck, with the mountain bike in the back, was gone!

It was a good five miles to town. At this hour of the night traffic rarely came down the road. Since it was government land there were no houses, either. Kader was looking at an hour and a half walk.

"Blast it!" Kader cried angrily.

Then, from nowhere, came the ghost biker streaking towards Kader, riding hard, hovering over the handlebars. Kader turned and started to run, but the bike was bearing down hard. The biker then ground to a stop, sending gravel in all directions. Kader stumbled on a rock as he tried to scramble to safety, and that was all he remembered. He struck the ground, losing consciousness.

Kader lay in the brush stunned for a few minutes. He'd knocked the wind out of himself. Now, slowly, he got to his feet. He heard an owl from somewhere. He remembered the biker and a bolt of fear ran through him. Was the guy still around?

Kader got up and brushed the dirt off his clothing. He didn't hear the sound of the pickaxe anymore. He didn't hear the shoveling. The ghost biker—whoever he was—was gone.

Kader started walking down the

dark road, hoping against hope somebody would come along to give him a lift so he wouldn't have to walk the entire five miles.

The moon wove in and out of clouds in the sky, turning the road light, then dark. Kader wished he had his mountain bike. He'd cover the distance easily then. But the bike was gone, and his pickup was gone.

Kader began to feel like a fool. He should have quit the mountain like everybody said. He should have left Coyote Mountain to the ghost biker. Even now the hairs on the back of his neck stood up in anger against doing that.

Chapter 7

Kader trudged down the road, his legs aching. It was near dawn and the sky was turning red when Kader reached the sheriff's office.

Kader stumbled into the sheriff's office and told Deputy Walsh everything that happened. "I think the guy is burying something up there. He was afraid I'd stumble on his dirty work," Kader said.

"Come on," the deputy said. "Climb in my truck. We'll go up there and take a look."

Kader got in beside the deputy, and they drove back to the spot where Kader had left his pickup and found it missing. To his shock it was sitting there where he left it, and the mountain bike was in the back, untouched.

"I thought you said somebody ripped off your truck, son," Deputy Walsh said.

"They did. I guess they drove it down the road and then returned it or something," Kader said.

"Well, let's see that fellow you say is digging up the mountain," the deputy said with a wry smile. Kader could tell he wasn't buying much of his story. It all did sound farfetched. The deputy didn't see the ghost biker with his horrifying white face. He didn't get a note saying keep off Coyote Mountain.

"I don't hear any pickaxe hitting the ground," the deputy said.

"He was digging right over there ... in that direction," Kader said.

The deputy made a quick walk around the brush. Maybe he missed the spot where the man had been digging.

Maybe the ghost biker had dragged brush over the spot to conceal it. It seemed pretty clear to Kader that the deputy didn't come out here to find something. He came out to satisfy Kader and try to make the boy see that it was all his imagination.

"Look, son, I'm sure some old biker dog menaced you. Just for fun probably. Thought it'd be funny to hassle a kid, especially a kid from another country. But I don't think it was much more than that. He's probably moved on to new digs. I don't think he'll be bothering you anymore. So let's just call it a day, okay?" the deputy said.

"You don't believe a word of what I've told you," Kader said bitterly.

"Sure I do," Deputy Walsh said, scratching his bald head and grinning in a friendly way. "A white faced ghost with black clothing riding a mountain bike chased you down and is digging away on the mountain. Look, son, why don't you go home and have a good breakfast and get to school. Maybe you can write this all up in your English class. I'll bet you'd get an A for it."

The deputy followed Kader back to town as Kader drove his pickup. His parents were alarmed over his absence. His mother was crying.

Kader explained everything that happened.

"Kader," Dad said firmly, "this family wants no more trouble! Stay off Coyote Mountain. As your father I order you to stay away from that place."

"I will, Dad," Kader promised, "but it makes me so mad that that guy is getting away with whatever he's doing up there. I couldn't believe how the deputy just laughed it all off."

"Justice will be done if he's a criminal," Kader's mother said, "but it's not your duty to do it. Thank God you were not hurt last night. We survived persecution and war in our homeland.

We didn't come to America to lose a precious son because of a crazy mountain!"

"I promise I won't go back there, Mom," Kader said, hugging his crying mother. "At least, not until it's perfectly safe again."

Chapter 8

"It's all like a bad dream," Kader told Paloma at school. "My head is spinning. I keep seeing this strange man with the white face and the dark clothes, but nobody else sees him. Nobody else believes he exists. I'm beginning to doubt myself!"

"I don't doubt you," Paloma said. "I trust you, Kader. You are the only solid thing in my life. Last night my parents fought all through dinner. Dad stalked off then. He slammed the door and made the whole house shake. He didn't even come home for breakfast. Mom says if things don't get better she will leave him."

"I'm sorry, Paloma," Kader said,

grateful for his own parents who'd come through so much turmoil still loving one another.

"Hey," a boy called to Kader, "everybody's saying you see ghosts up on Coyote Mountain. Is that true?"

"What do the ghosts look like, Kader?" another boy yelled. "Do they look like they're wearing bed sheets?"

One of the laughing boys was Deputy Walsh's son. Kader didn't have to wonder where the stories had come from.

"Do the ghosts go boooooo?" asked Jeremy Walsh.

"Get lost," Kader snapped.

"Awww … he's so sensitive," Jeremy laughed louder.

"Don't mind them," Paloma said, patting Kader's hand. "I believe every word you said, Kader. Something bad is going on up on Coyote Mountain."

When Kader got home he found Najor shooting baskets. Najor usually got home from school a few minutes earlier than Kader.

"Want to play some one on one?" Kader asked his younger brother.

"Yeah, sure!" Najor grinned.

They played for several minutes with Najor holding his own surprisingly well. "You just might make a basketball player someday after all," Kader said.

"You think so? Man, that'd be great," Najor said. "When I see you getting ready for practice I envy you so much."

"The guys at school are giving me a hard time about me seeing that ghost biker on Coyote Mountain," Kader said.

"Why don't you just forget all about that old mountain and think about the basketball season? I looked in an old history book and read that six guys died up on Coyote Mountain in the 1870s or something. There was a big gunfight between two gangs," Najor said. "Maybe the spirits of those dead crooks are roaming around."

Kader glanced towards the street as a bike streaked by. It had markings just like the ghost biker's mountain bike. "Hey," Kader yelled, "I think that's the guy's bike!"

"You mean the one that just went by?" Najor said.

"Yeah," Kader said, running to his own bike and jumping on. "I promised Mom and Dad I wouldn't go back to Coyote Mountain, but I'm going to find out who's riding that bike."

Kader gained on the bike at the next corner and gasped. Paloma was riding the bike! He hadn't recognized her with her dark hair tucked into a red cap, wearing her father's leather jacket.

"Paloma," Kader yelled, "that's not your bike you're riding. Where did you get that bike?"

Paloma stopped and smiled at Kader. "You scared me when you

started yelling. My father bought this bike from some guy—he traded my blue bike. Why? What's the matter, Kader?"

"I think that bike belonged to the guy who chased me off Coyote Mountain, Paloma. Do you mind if I go over to your house and ask your Dad who sold him the bike?"

Paloma stared at him, wide-eyed, shaking her head.

Chapter 9

Kader and Paloma rode together to Paloma's house. The Halloween and jewelry stores were on the ground floor. The family lived upstairs.

"I hope Dad came home," Paloma said. "I hope they're not fighting right now. It embarrasses me so much when they fight in front of my friends."

Kader followed Paloma into the Halloween store. The walls were hung with spooky masks, shrunken heads, coconut shells carved into monkey faces, and holiday decorations. Paloma's father stood behind the counter. Paloma breathed a sigh of relief. "Hi, Dad. Kader wanted to ask you about the new bike you bought for me, the silver one," Paloma said.

"What about it, Kader?" Paloma's father asked.

"Well, this guy who's been harassing me up on Coyote Mountain. It looks like his bike. Maybe you got the bike from him," Kader said. "He's a tall, gaunt guy who dresses in black, and he's got white makeup or something on his face."

Paloma's father nodded. "I believe that would aptly describe the fellow I bought the bike from. A drifter. He was going down the road in a truck and the bike was in the back. It looked like a nice bike, and I wanted a better one for Paloma. I hope the bike wasn't stolen or anything." Paloma's father was a thin, weary-looking man. He had had many jobs and several businesses, and all of them had been failures. Now, he looked like he carried the weight of the world on his shoulders. "Oh, dear ... don't tell me I've made another stupid mistake," he lamented.

Paloma's mother came into the store. She heard the last part of the conversation and her expression turned bitter. "You fouled up again, Frederick? Well, it's not surprising. I've lost count of the times you have fouled up."

Kader felt sorry for the tall, broken man. He didn't look well. Deep circles underscored his eyes. His skin had an unhealthy orange pallor as if he had liver trouble. "It wasn't a mistake that you bought the bike, sir," Kader said. "It might even lead me to the guy I'm after. So, you say he was driving a pickup truck?"

"Yes. New Jersey plates. He said something about leaving the area and going to Newark," Paloma's father said.

"You didn't happen to notice if he had a pickaxe and shovels in the back of the pickup, did you?" Kader asked.

"Mmmm ... as a matter of fact, yes he did. I ... ah ... asked him what his profession was. He said he was a grave digger. I laughed at that. And the fellow said, 'I bury dreams'. And then he said, 'Before men die, their dreams die. That's why a dream-burying man is so important'."

"What nonsense," Paloma's mother scoffed. "Isn't it just like you to take up with such a fool."

"Thanks, sir," Kader said to Paloma's father. Then, as Kader and Paloma walked out of the store together, Kader said, "I guess that settles the mystery, doesn't it? Some weirdo just camped out on the mountain for a few weeks, and he wanted to keep everybody else off it."

"Yeah," Paloma said. "I'm glad he's gone."

"Me, too. I guess I can go back to my mountain then," Kader said.

"Things can be like they were before," Paloma said. Her eyes were sad with a kind of longing. "Kader, when

I was little there was happiness in our house. We all hoped for better times. Now ... well ..."

"See you at school, Paloma," Kader said, kissing her dusky cheek.

Chapter 10

Kader biked home. The whole Toma family sat down to dinner together. At last they were prosperous enough to hire help in the deli, so a family member didn't always have to be on duty. Now they could occasionally have a family meal together.

"I guess I'll never find out what the guy was doing on Coyote Mountain," Kader said.

"Probably looking for gold," Dad said. "I think bandits hid gold up there years ago."

"I suppose some drifter heard about that and thought he could discover some lost treasure," Kader said. "I still sorta wish I could have seen the guy and proved to myself and everybody else that he really existed. Then I could really close the door on the whole thing."

"Some doors must always stay open a crack," Mom said. "We never learn the truth in the world."

"I guess so," Kader said. But that night in bed he tossed and turned with nightmares about the ghost biker. Suddenly, around midnight, Kader sat up in bed, his heart pounding. He knew who the mountain biker, who'd chased him from Coyote Mountain, was. He knew who the white-faced desperado was.

After school on Thursday, Kader biked to the Halloween store run by Paloma's parents. He walked in to find Paloma's father working over the books. Kader moved slowly down the rows of masks until he found the ghost biker's face.

"This is the mask the ghost biker

wore," Kader said.

Paloma's father got up slowly. "Yes," he said.

Kader stood there in silence, waiting for the man to continue speaking. When he did it was with a heavy voice and labored breathing.

"This fellow who wore the mask and threatened you, Kader ... he was a desperate man. He was a truly desperate man. He read in an old magazine that some bandit had left gold coins up on Coyote Mountain and nobody had ever found them. For this poor desperate fool it seemed a final chance to reclaim his life from total failure."

"I see," Kader said.

"He wanted some dignity ... some small measure of success. He meant you no harm, Kader. He just thought you too might discover the gold just as he was about to snatch wealth from the jaws of poverty. Of course, the poor wretch found no gold."

"None at all?" Kader asked.

"No, nothing." The man turned and looked right at Kader. "And this man, this fool, he wanted one final chance to be somebody in the eyes of his wife, his daughters."

Kader nodded.

"So, Kader, it's up to you. Shall we call the police? I will confess to all the mischief I caused, of course."

Kader shook his head. "I think the ghost biker who threatened me went to New Jersey like you said, sir. I think we'll just leave it at that."

Paloma's father nodded, a thin smile trembling on his lips.

"Sir, don't stop dreaming," Kader said. "There still could be a rainbow, you know. I mean, you can't really bury dreams. They're like seeds. They keep on sprouting."

"Thank you, Kader," the man said.

Kader biked home. All of a sudden the load lifted from his shoulders.

Kader was actually looking forward to the start of tomorrow's basketball game. But then, on his first free afternoon he'd be back on Coyote Mountain, streaking down the trail, showing his mud-caked grin to the yellow mustard on the hills.